This book belongs to

....
....

for Mum and Dad
and a Thankyou
to Naia*
(and Adrienne)

DK

www.dk.com

First published in Great Britain in 1999
by Dorling Kindersley Limited,
9 Henrietta Street, London WC2E 8PS

2 4 6 8 10 9 7 5 3 1

Copyright © 1999 Jane Cabrera
The author and illustrator's moral rights have been asserted.

A CIP catalogue record for this book is available from the British Library.

ISBN 0-7513-7168-8 (Hardback)
ISBN 0-7513-6242-5 (Paperback)

Colour reproduction by Dot Gradations, UK
Printed in Hong Kong by Wing King Tong

☆ Starring Jerry-lee Johnson & Rowan Kirby Brown

Rory
and
the
Lion

Jane Cabrera

Rory loved lions.

His favourite game was the lion game.
Rory put on his lion costume and
roared as loudly as he could.
"I'm **Roary** the lion!"

Roar
Roar!

Then one night, Rory
heard a real lion roar.
He ran to the window
but the lion had gone.

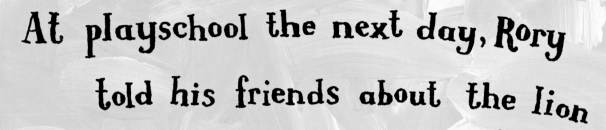

At playschool the next day, Rory
told his friends about the lion
he had heard in the night.
"Don't be silly," they said.
"Lions don't live here."

After school, Rory and Su passed a field of cows. "Moo," went the cow. "Maybe that's the noise you heard," said Su.

Moo!

But that night Rory heard the lion roar again.

The next day, Rory
went to Max's farm.
"Oink," grunted a pig.
"Is that what you
heard?" Max asked.

OINK!

But it wasn't.
Rory heard the lion
roar again that night.
This time he roared back.

On Thursday, Rory and Rowan saw a horse.

"Neigh," went the horse.

"Is that what you heard?" Rowan asked.

On Friday, Rory
played at Jerry-Lee's house.
"Woof," barked his dog, Tommy.
"Perhaps that's the noise you
heard," said Jerry-Lee.

WOOF!

That night, when Rory heard the lion, he roared back as loudly as he could.

On Saturday,
Rory was playing in the
garden when he heard the roar again.
He prowled towards the noise until Rory
Knew the lion was right behind the bush.

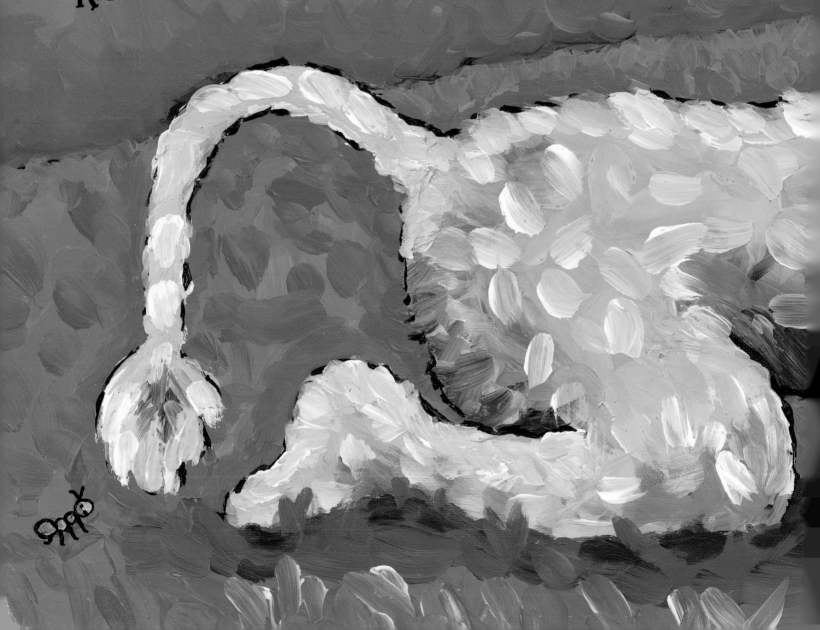

ROAR!

Quietly
he crept
round it
and there was...

...another boy!
"So you're the lion,"
they both said together.
And then they laughed
and let out an enormous...

RO

Leo

Other Toddler Books to collect:

*

BALL! by Ros Asquith, illustrated by Sam Williams

PANDA BIG AND PANDA SMALL by Jane Cabrera

CATERPILLAR'S WISH by Mary Murphy

I'M TOO BUSY by Helen Stephens

WHAT ABOUT ME? by Helen Stephens

THE PIG WHO WISHED by Joyce Dunbar, illustrated by Selina Young

BABY LOVES by Michael Lawrence, illustrated by Adrian Reynolds

SILLY GOOSE AND DAFT DUCK PLAY HIDE-AND-SEEK
by Sally Grindley, illustrated by Adrian Reynolds

HIDE AND SLEEP by Melanie Walsh

TING-A-LING! by Siobhan Dodds

GRANDMA RABBITTY'S VISIT by Barry Smith